BLOOMFIELD TOWNSHIP PUBLIC LIBRARY
3 1160 00438 9271

D1075170

Close Call

Close Call

Todd Strasser

G. P. Putnam's Sons
New York

G. P. Putnam's Sons, a division of Penguin Putnam Books for Young Readers,
345 Hudson Street, New York, NY 10014.
G. P. Putnam's Sons, Reg. U.S. Pat. & Tm. Off.
Published simultaneously in Canada.
Printed in the United States of America.
Book designed by Tony Sahara. Text set in Minion.
Library of Congress Cataloging-in-Publication Data
Strasser, Todd.
Close call/by Todd Strasser. p. cm.
Summary: A group of fifth and sixth graders find a way to deal
with personal differences, family problems, and some rock-
throwing high school boys so that they can play the game they love.
ISBN 0-399-23134-X
[1. Frindship—Ficiton. 2. Baseball—Fiction.] I. Title.
PZ7.S899C1 1999
[Fic]—dc21 98-36947 CIP AC
1 3 5 7 9 10 8 6 4 2
First Impression

To the 1998 Larchmont Comets:

Jimmy Anderson, Antoine Cochennec, Alex Cowen,
Neal Ferrick, Raymond Feuga, Samuel Hamilton,
Alex Janoff, Owen Joyce, Alexander Kent, Gregory Kent,
Cody Lister, Max St. Denis, Nicholas Stelluti,
Brendon Stiffle, Geoffrey Strasser, and Craig Weinrib

For being good sports
while always playing their hardest.

Close Call

Chapter 1

Crack! The ball came off Stuart Feng's bat and shot down the third baseline. Stuart bolted toward first. Out of the corner of his eye he saw the ball hit the ground and bounce over third base.

Stuart was a wiry boy with black hair. He smiled to himself as he ran. It was definitely a double. And maybe, if he really hustled, he could stretch it into a triple.

"Foul!" a voice shouted.

Huh!? Stuart skidded to a stop and stared across the baseball diamond at Jenny Long, who was playing third base for the opposing team. She was the one who'd called the ball foul.

"What did you say?" Stuart wondered if he'd heard wrong.

"I said, 'Foul!' " answered Jenny. She was an average-size girl with brown hair and freckles.

"Are you crazy?" Stuart yelled.

"It was fair!" insisted Krishnan Mehta, the captain of Stuart's team. She started to jog from the backstop to third base. Krishnan was a tall girl with long black hair pulled into a pony tail. She had olive-colored skin and dark eyes.

"I saw it foul." Jenny crossed her arms stubbornly.

"You're blind!" Stuart shouted. "The ball bounced right over the base! It was totally and completely one hundred-fifteen percent fair!"

"Was not," Jenny insisted.

"Was too!" Stuart joined Krishnan. They both stopped in front of Jenny.

"Jenny, the ball was fair," Krishnan said calmly. "It really was. I was standing right on the third base line. I saw it."

"Well, I saw it foul," Jenny replied. "So tough luck."

Stuart couldn't believe it! No way was he going to let Jenny rob him of that hit. He yanked the ragged Florida Marlins cap off his head and slammed it to the ground.

"You're crazy!" he yelled. "The ball was fair. It's tough luck on *you!*"

In center field, Ian Piccolo slowly chewed a piece of stale bubble gum and watched them argue. Ian was a tall, slender boy with reddish-brown hair and pale skin. He was the captain of Jenny's team.

At third base the argument continued. Krishnan spoke calmly to Jenny. Jenny kept shaking her head. Stuart kept yelling and jumping up and down on his baseball cap.

Ian cracked his gum and gazed around the dusty high school ball field. It wasn't much more than some bases and a rusty old backstop. The outfield was also used for soccer and football. Here and there a weed sprouted up through the hard-packed earth. When they played ball, no one worried about getting grass stains on their school clothes.

Beyond the ball field was the town and then streets lined with parked cars and rows of small brick houses pressed tightly together. Beyond that were a few low apartment buildings.

Ian and his friends were mostly fifth and sixth graders. While waiting for the argument at third base to end, they stood with their hands on their hips, or pounded their fists into their gloves. The players on Krishnan's team stood around the backstop cracking gum and taking practice swings. Like Ian, they just wanted to get on with the game.

But the argument only seemed to be growing worse. Now Stuart and Jenny were both yelling while Krishnan stood by and watched helplessly. Ian was always amazed by how serious these games got. After all, they were just a bunch of kids. They came in shorts and T-shirts, or jeans and long sleeves, wearing baseball caps from a dozen different major league teams.

"The ball was fair!" Stuart screamed. By now he'd stomped his cap so many times it had almost disappeared into the dirt.

"It's my call!" Jenny yelled back.

"It's stupid to fight," pleaded Krishnan.

Crash! The sound of breaking glass yanked Ian's attention away from the argument. Over in the high school parking lot some older kids were smoking cigarettes and breaking bottles.

Ian felt his stomach tighten. The older kids made him nervous. Sometimes, when they got bored and had nothing better to do, they threw rocks at the ball players. But Ian and his friends loved playing baseball. So they came back to the high school field day after day, even though the older kids scared them.

"I saw it fair and Krishnan saw it fair!" Stuart's shrill voice rose above the others. "That's two against one!"

Out on the field, Tameka Williams, the short stop on Ian's team, gave Ian a questioning look. He knew what she was thinking: *When was he going to break up the fight so that they could get on with the game?*

Ian sighed, straightened his cap, and started toward third base. It looked like he would have to break it up. Otherwise the game might never get going again.

Chapter 2

"Did you see the ball?" Stuart asked when Ian joined the group.

"From where I was I couldn't see if it was fair or foul," Ian answered truthfully.

"Krishnan was right on the third baseline and she says it was fair," Stuart said.

"Of course she said that," Jenny countered. "She's the captain of your team, Stuart. She wants the ball to be fair."

"If I saw it foul I would say so," Krishnan insisted.

"Yeah, right." Jenny smirked and rolled her eyes in disbelief.

Tameka joined them. She had long, shining relaxed black hair, big brown eyes, and an ever-present smile.

"Here's an amazing idea!" she announced. "Let's have a do-over!"

"No way!" Stuart cried. "That's totally not fair. I could have had a double. Maybe even a triple! Having a do-over is the same as saying the ball was foul."

He looked to Ian for support.

"All I know is it's going to be dark soon," Ian said. Behind him, the sun hovered above the old brick high school, throwing a long, dark shadow across the outfield. "And then it's not going to matter what the ball was."

"Tell you what," Stuart said to Jenny. "I know I could have stretched that hit into a triple, but I'll settle for a double. Okay? That's a good compromise."

"It was foul," Jenny insisted again.

"It was fair," said Krishnan.

"It's two against one," Ian said to Jenny. "And Stuart said he'd compromise."

"I don't care if it's ten *thousand* against one," Jenny shot back. "I was the closest to the ball and I saw it foul."

"Amazing idea number two," said Tameka. "Why don't you shoot for it?"

"Fine." Stuart pulled his hand back in a fist. "I've got odds."

But Jenny shook her head and kept her arms crossed.

"Come on, Jenny," Tameka urged her. "Just shoot for it. Everyone wants to play."

"No. I always lose," Jenny argued.

"We'll make it two out of three," Stuart offered.

"No! I saw it foul!" Jenny's voice cracked. She turned to Ian with watery eyes. "Why don't you believe me?"

Ian and the others were surprised to see tears in Jenny's eyes. Why was she taking this so seriously?

"It's just a baseball game, Jenny," Krishnan said softly.

But Jenny had had enough. Everyone was against her.

"I hate you!" she yelled at them, then turned and started to run away. "I hate *all* of you!"

Chapter 3

They all watched as Jenny ran across the field and toward the street.

"What's with her?" Tameka asked.

No one answered. Stuart bent down and picked up his dirty cap. Now he felt bad. Dusting off the cap, he turned to his friends. "Listen, guys, I am absolutely, positively, one hundred twenty-five percent sure that ball was fair."

"We know, Stuart," Krishnan assured him.

Meanwhile, the rest of the baseball players were still waiting.

"Are we gonna play or what?" called Richie Perez. Richie was tall and broad-shouldered with dark hair and dark eyes.

Krishnan turned to Ian. "What should we do?"

Ian cracked his gum and looked around. *Why,* he wondered, *did they always aim the big questions at me?* At school his teacher, Ms. Jackson, once told him he had "leadership qualities." But just what those qualities were, or how he came to have them, was a mystery to him.

The sun had now dropped behind the high school. The long, deep shadow had crept onto the baseball diamond. It was Friday and the weekend was here, which meant they'd have a lot more chances to play baseball.

Over in the parking lot, the high school kids were looking in their direction. The biggest kid had short blond hair, tattoos and gold hoops in his ears. His name was Billy and he was Jenny's stepbrother. Ian had seen him selling cherry bombs, cigarettes, and plastic cigarette lighters to younger kids.

Ian looked back at the ball players. Now that Jenny had run away, he only had six players on his team. Krishnan had seven. There was no one to take Jenny's place at third.

"Let's call it," Ian said with a shrug.

Krishnan turned to the others. "Game's over."

Not all the players picked up their school packs and

left the field. Richie Perez and a few other die-hards said they were going to stay and take turns batting and fielding until it got too dark to see.

Sometimes Ian was one of the die-hards. There were days when he felt like he couldn't get enough baseball. But after that fight with Jenny, this wasn't going to be one of them.

He started to walk home with Stuart, Krishnan and Tameka. To avoid the high school kids, they ducked through a hole in the right field fence. They walked through town, passing the stores, post office and market. The town was old and most of the buildings were made of brick. None of them were very tall.

"What's with Jenny?" Tameka asked.

"She did the same thing last week," Krishnan reminded them. "With the double play, remember?"

Ian had to think back for a moment. They'd played three or four games in the past week and each one had had a few disagreements.

"I remember," Tameka recalled. "The one where she insisted she was safe."

"Right," Stuart said. "And she was out by a mile."

"At least she didn't run away that time," said Krishnan.

"She just argued and argued until we gave up and let her stay on base," said Tameka.

"It was a blowout anyway," Stuart said. "The other team was winning by so much it didn't matter whether she scored or not."

"So what's your point?" Ian asked Krishnan.

Krishnan swept back her long, straight black hair. "Just that she didn't used to be this way. I mean, I don't ever remember her arguing last year."

Now instead of trying to think back one week, everyone tried to think back one year. But as best as they could recall, Jenny never used to argue or fight over calls. This was something new.

They passed the last of the stores in town. Ahead of them were blocks of houses bunched tightly together. In front of some of the houses were kick balls and tricycles. Nubs of colored chalk lay on the front walks where little kids had drawn stick figures and names.

It was a warm spring evening and some grown-ups were sitting on their stoops or porches. People pushed mowers across their lawns or gardened in flower beds.

Across the street, a lady with red hair was walking five dogs on long leashes. The kids called her the five-dog lady. She was always out with her dogs when they came home from their baseball games.

“Here’s my last amazing idea of the day,” said Tameka. “Before the next game, let’s talk about the rules. Let’s decide who is supposed to make the calls and what we’ll do when there’s an argument.”

“Sounds good,” Stuart said.

Ian agreed. But inside, he wasn’t so sure.

Chapter 4

That night Krishnan ate dinner at Ian's house. Krishnan's parents ran a small store that sold newspapers, candy and lottery tickets. On Fridays and Saturdays both of her parents worked until midnight, so Krishnan often ate dinner at her friends' houses.

"Thanks for letting me eat over, Mrs. Piccolo," Krishnan said as she and Ian set the dinner table.

"You don't have to thank me," replied Ian's mother as she stood at the stove, stirring a pot of spaghetti and warming some tomato sauce. Her name was Karen and she worked as a visiting nurse. "I like having Ian's friends over. It's the only way I ever find out what's going on in his life."

Ian gave his mom a look. She winked back, but he knew she was being serious.

"So how was school today?" Mrs. Piccolo asked.

"Who remembers?" Ian replied.

"See what I mean?" his mom said to Krishnan. Then she looked at her son. "I bet you remember every hit you got in your baseball game *after* school."

Ian did. But he also remembered the weird way Jenny had acted. He glanced at Krishnan and had the feeling that she was thinking the same thing.

"Pretty quiet tonight," Mrs. Piccolo said from the stove.

Ian stared down at the plates and silverware he and Krishnan had just placed on the table.

"Something wrong?" his mom asked.

"Jenny Long's been acting weird," Ian said.

"In what way?" Mrs. Piccolo asked.

"Arguing over dumb stuff, quitting the game and running away," Ian said.

Before Mrs. Piccolo could respond, Ian's little brother Tommy came into the kitchen. Tommy was six and in first grade. He refused to dress in anything except green and brown army camouflage clothes. Today he was wearing a camouflage hat, camouflage long sleeve shirt, camouflage pants and green boots. Around his waist was an green army belt with a canteen and a holster with a toy pistol.

"Uh oh," Ian chuckled. "It's the Mad Bomber."

"Please don't call him that," Mrs. Piccolo said.

"I need matches," Tommy said.

"Why?" replied his mother.

Tommy held up a small black plastic grenade with a red fuse sticking out of it.

The worry lines in Mrs. Piccolo's forehead bunched up. "What is that?"

"A bomb," Tommy said. "Ricky Leeds gave it to me."

"Will it explode?" Mrs. Piccolo asked.

"Oh, yeah," Tommy nodded eagerly. "It makes a big explosion. And a lot of smoke."

"Then I don't want you playing with it." Mrs. Piccolo held out her hand. "Give it to me, Tommy."

"No!" Tommy backed away and hid the grenade behind his back. "It's mine!"

"It's dangerous, Tommy," Mrs. Piccolo said. "You can't have it."

"It's not that dangerous," Ian said.

"Is, too!" Tommy insisted.

"It's just a smoke bomb," said Ian. "I used to play with them all the time. You light it and some smoke comes out. That's all."

"That's a lie!" Tommy yelled. "Ricky said it'll blow up a whole car!"

"A car?" Mrs. Piccolo frowned.

"Don't your parents sell them at the store?" Ian asked Krishnan.

"I think so," she answered.

Ian turned to his mother. "You really think they'd sell something that could blow up a car?"

"Darn right!" Tommy exclaimed, but Mrs. Piccolo seemed to relax.

"All right," she said. "We'll go outside after dinner and I'll light it on the sidewalk. Now sit down and have dinner, Tommy."

Tommy sat down across from Krishnan.

"How come your skin is so dark?" he asked.

"It's none of your business," Ian snapped.

"It's okay," Krishnan said. "It's because I'm Indian."

Tommy's eyebrows rose. "Like Cowboys and Indians?"

"No, dummy, like from the country of India," Ian corrected him.

"Ian," Mrs. Piccolo said sternly, "don't call your brother a dummy."

"Where's the country of India?" Tommy asked.

"Far away," said Ian.

"Farther than the mall?" Tommy asked.

"Farther than Disney World," Krishnan said with a smile.

Tommy frowned. "What are you doing in this country?"

"My parents came here when they were young," Krishnan said.

"Do they have army men in India?" Tommy asked.

"I don't know," Krishnan said. "I guess."

Mrs. Piccolo brought a steaming bowl of spaghetti over to the table. They started to eat. Besides the spaghetti, there was garlic bread and steamed broccoli.

"Great garlic bread, Mrs. Piccolo," Krishnan said.

"Thank you," said Mrs. Piccolo. "Now you were saying something before about a friend who was acting strange. . ."

"Jenny Long," Ian said. "She keeps fighting with everyone."

"Why don't you blow her up?" Tommy asked.

"Why don't you shut up?" Ian snapped.

"Don't talk that way to your brother," Mrs. Piccolo scolded Ian, then patiently said to Tommy, "That's not the way we solve our problems, hon."

Ian's mom turned again to Ian and Krishnan. "It sounds like something must be bothering her. Why don't you ask her what's wrong."

"It's hard, Mom," Ian said. "Everyone wants to play baseball. They don't want to sit around and talk."

"Then don't do it at a game," Mrs. Piccolo said. "Do it at another time. Maybe at school."

"And if she still argues," Tommy added, "*then* blow her up!"

Chapter 5

Over the weekend, Jenny didn't come to a single game. Ian knew that wasn't normal. At lunch in school on Monday, she wanted to know how many times they'd played and what had happened.

"They were just regular games," Ian said.

"Oh, come on," Jenny practically begged. "Tell me."

"Richie hit two home runs," said Tameka.

"I had a double play at second," Stuart said proudly.

"Big deal," Tameka sniggered. "You caught the ball and stepped on the bag. If Ian hadn't taken such a long lead, it never would have happened."

"Hey! The reason Ian took that lead was because he didn't think I had a chance," Stuart defended himself.

"The reason I took that lead was because I thought there were two outs when there was only one," Ian corrected him.

Everyone laughed, including Jenny.

• • •

The next time they played after school was on Tuesday. When Ian got to the ball field he was glad Jenny was there. The problem was, hardly anyone else showed up. There weren't enough kids for two teams.

"Where is everyone?" Jenny asked.

"Richie had to stay after school for a second," Krishnan answered.

Tameka and Stuart added that they knew a few kids who were on their way.

"Anyone want to have a catch?" Ian asked.

"I want to play," Jenny said impatiently.

"We will," Krishnan assured her. "As soon as enough kids get here."

They started to throw the ball around. Stuart threw it to Ian.

Plap! The ball hit Ian's mitt. He threw it to Jenny.

Plap! Jenny caught the ball. She rolled her eyes and shook her head, as if letting everyone know she thought it was dumb. Then she threw the ball to Tameka.

"I can't believe it," Jenny muttered. "I finally get to play and no one's here."

Krishnan gave Ian a look. For a second Ian didn't know what it meant. Then he realized she was asking if this was a good time to talk to Jenny about the rules. It probably was, but Ian didn't know where or how to begin.

Plap! The ball came to Krishnan, but instead of throwing it to someone else, she held onto it and turned to Jenny.

"We want to talk to you," she said.

"Why?" Jenny's eyes darted around at Ian, Stuart and Tameka. "What about?"

"The rules," Tameka said.

"So we don't have the same problem we had last Friday," added Stuart.

"I know the rules," Jenny said with a huff. "If the ball bounces over the base, it's fair. But that ball was foul."

"That's not what we meant," Tameka said.

"We want to talk about what we'll do if something like that happens again," Krishnan explained, "so we can take care of it and get back to the game."

Jenny shook her head. "This is dumb."

"No, arguing about calls is dumb," countered Stuart.

"Let's just play," Jenny said impatiently. "I didn't get to play all weekend."

"First we should agree on what we'll do next time," Tameka said.

"Agree on this, agree on that, tell your mother she's getting fat." Jenny made up a rhyme, then turned and started to walk away.

Behind her, Ian, Krishnan, Stuart and Tameka shared a frustrated look.

"From now on we'll always have a do-over when we can't agree on a call," Stuart called loudly.

"Whatever," Jenny replied with a shrug.

Chapter 6

It wasn't long before enough kids had arrived for a game, and they chose up sides and started to play. Tameka and Krishnan were captains. Jenny was on Tameka's team, along with Ian.

By the top of the fourth inning, the game was tied three to three. Jenny was the lead-off batter.

Ian stood with Tameka behind the backstop while Jenny stepped up to the plate.

On the pitcher's mound, Stuart wound up and threw.

Jenny took a big swing . . . and missed.

"You don't have to blast it out of the park, Jenny," Tameka said. "All we need is a hit."

Stuart wound up and threw again.

The pitch was too low.

At the very last second, Jenny took another big cut at the ball . . . and missed.

Ian grimaced.

"Why'd she swing at *that?*" Tameka whispered.

"Come on, Jenny," Ian called. "Wait for your pitch. Just make contact and get on base."

Stuart's next pitch was right down the middle. If Ian had been at bat, he would have crushed the ball.

Jenny let it go by.

"Looks like it's one of those days," Tameka groaned softly.

On the pitcher's mound, Stuart wound up and threw again. The pitch was too high. Jenny swung and missed.

"Strike three!" Stuart let out a whoop and raised his fist in triumph. "You're out!"

Instead of leaving the batter's box, Jenny set up for another pitch.

Stuart stopped celebrating and frowned. "What are you doing?"

"Foul tip." Jenny twisted her feet in the dirt and brought the bat back over her shoulder.

"No way!" Stuart cried. "You missed it by a mile."

“Did not.” Jenny didn’t budge from the batter’s box.

Stuart turned to Tameka and Ian. “Did you guys hear a foul tip?”

Ian and Tameka shook their heads. Like Stuart, they were sure Jenny had missed the ball.

Stuart turned back to Jenny. “See? Even your own team says you’re out.”

Jenny just shook her head. “Foul tip.”

Stuart stood on the pitcher’s mound with his hands on his hips and glowered at her. “You’re out, Jenny. You’re not getting another pitch.”

“Well, I’m not leaving the batter’s box,” Jenny countered.

They’d reached a stalemate.

“Here we go again,” Tameka muttered to Ian and started out onto the field.

Chapter 7

Ian walked with Tameka. Krishnan came over from second base. They all met at the pitcher's mound.

"That was no foul tip!" Stuart insisted, getting excited as usual.

"We know," Tameka replied quietly. She didn't want Jenny to hear.

"So she's out," Stuart said.

Ian glanced at Jenny in the batter's box. She was in her batting stance—knees slightly bent, bat hovering above her shoulder—waiting for the next pitch.

He turned back to Stuart. "Remember what we said before? If we can't agree, it'll be a do-over."

"That's right," Krishnan agreed. Since she was the captain of Stuart's team, that should have settled the problem.

Ian and Tameka started to walk back to the back stop. Krishnan started back to second base.

"Wait a minute," Stuart said.

Everyone stopped.

"That means I have to throw Jenny another pitch," Stuart said. "That's just like saying it was a foul tip. So it's not really a do-over. It's really Jenny getting her way."

At home plate, Jenny smiled as if she'd known that all along.

"You see!?" Stuart cried. "It's not fair! She tricked us!"

"Hey, I didn't make the rule," Jenny said. "You guys did."

Ian, Tameka and Krishnan shared a frustrated look. They'd tried to make a rule so that the game wouldn't get bogged down by arguments. But now the game was getting bogged down by an argument over the rule!

"Just throw another pitch," Ian told Stuart.

Stuart squinted angrily at Jenny. He blew a bubble and cracked it. He slid his mitt under his arm and rubbed the baseball with both hands. He knew Jenny was cheating, but the truth was he was tired of arguing, too. He waited until everyone was in position, then wound up and threw.

Jenny took another big swing . . . and missed.

Stuart grinned with satisfaction. This time he'd struck her out for sure.

Instead of leaving the batter's box, Jenny pulled the bat back and waited for another pitch.

Stuart's jaw dropped. "Now what?"

"Foul tip," Jenny replied with a grin.

"No way!?" Stuart slammed his mitt to the ground. "That was no foul tip!" He pulled off his baseball cap and threw it to the ground, too. "You struck out fair and square!"

Jenny didn't budge.

"She's cheating!" Stuart's face turned red and he stamped his foot on the ground. "Don't you see what she's doing? She'll say every ball is a foul tip until she gets a hit."

Ian walked toward the batter's box.

"Come on, Jenny," he said. "You're out."

Jenny shook her head. "Foul tip."

"No, it wasn't," Ian said. "You struck out."

"Did not," Jenny insisted.

"Yes, you did," Ian replied firmly. He held out his hand. "Give me the bat."

Jenny squeezed the bat and rested it against her

shoulder. "You made a rule that any time there's a disagreement we'll have a do-over."

"Not this time," Ian said, still holding out his hand for the bat.

"But that's the rule you made," Jenny insisted.

Ian shook his head.

"Then you're the cheater." Jenny's face clouded over. She wasn't smiling anymore. "You're the one who doesn't play by the rules."

"Just give me the bat," Ian said calmly.

Jenny narrowed her eyes angrily. She dropped the bat on the ground. "You're just like everyone else," she grumbled. "You make rules and then break them when it suits you."

Ian frowned.

"What are you talking about, Jenny?" Tameka asked.

Jenny glared at them with eyes filled with anger. Instead of answering, she stomped away.

"Where are you going?" Krishnan called after her.

Jenny didn't answer. She started to run toward the right field fence.

"Hey, come back!" Tameka yelled.

But Jenny didn't stop. She left the field, turned the corner, and was gone.

A silence fell over the field.

"What's with her?" Stuart asked.

"You got me," said Tameka.

"She couldn't wait to play baseball today," Krishnan said. "I don't get it. Doesn't she know it's just a game?"

Ian blew a bubble, then let it deflate on its own. The truth was, baseball wasn't just a game. At least, not to him. It was more like a place. A place where there was no school, no problems, and no annoying little brothers. Sometimes you lost, and sometimes you won, but you almost always had fun. Just knowing baseball was there made it easier to deal with all the other hassles in life.

To Ian, there was no problem so big it could follow you onto the baseball field. He had always assumed that the rest of the ball players felt the same way. But now he was beginning to sense that might not be true.

Chapter 8

The next day at lunch, Jenny sat with them, talking and laughing, and acting as if nothing had happened the day before. The kids always ate as fast as they could. If it wasn't raining, after lunch they would go out to the schoolyard and play. One day it might be soccer, the next basketball or touch football.

Jenny finished lunch first and jumped up from the table. "See you guys outside."

Ian and the others watched her jog away through the crowded cafeteria.

"That was weird," said Tameka.

"You mean the way she acted?" Krishnan guessed. "Like yesterday never happened?"

"You got it," Tameka said.

"Are we gonna play after school today?" Stuart suddenly asked.

"I can," Tameka said.

"I'll be there," said Krishnan.

"Me, too," said Ian.

"Let's not tell Jenny, okay?" Stuart said. "Every time she plays, she ruins the game. All she does is fight."

For a moment, no one knew what to say. It was the first time Ian could remember someone suggesting one of their friends not be told about a game.

"But she always plays with us," Krishnan finally said.

"If we don't tell her, maybe she'll get the message," Stuart said, and started to get up. "Then next time she won't argue so much. See you guys later."

"Going outside?" Ian asked.

Stuart shook his head. "I'm going to the library. They've got a new baseball CD on the computer."

Stuart made his way through the cafeteria and left. Ian remained behind at the lunch table with Tameka and Krishnan.

"Jenny's going to be so mad when she finds out," Krishnan said.

"It's not right to keep her out of the game," said Ian.

"But if you tell her, than you'll get Stuart mad," Tameka said.

Krishnan wrinkled her forehead. "How did it get so complicated?"

"I don't know," Ian said with a weary shrug. "All we want to do is play ball."

• • •

When school ended, Ian and some of the other kids walked to the high school. They always carried their baseball gloves in their backpacks. At the field they chose up teams. Today Ian and Tameka were captains. Ian chose Stuart first because he was the best pitcher.

Tameka chose a stocky blond-haired boy named Bobby who played first base and hit well. Ian chose Richie Perez. Tameka chose Krishnan.

Ian knew if Jenny was around, he probably would have picked her next. He felt bad she wasn't there. He even glanced toward the street, hoping she might be on her way. But there was no sign of her, and Ian chose someone else. The game started and pretty soon Ian forgot about Jenny and everything else.

They had just finished the second inning. Ian was trotting out toward second base when Tameka stopped in front of him.

"Guess who's here?" she asked.

For a moment, Ian didn't understand what she was talking about. "Who?"

Tameka tilted her head toward the street. Jenny was standing at the fence.

Ian's eyes met Jenny's. He felt foolish and guilty, as if he'd been caught doing something wrong.

Jenny frowned. Then she turned away and walked quickly down the sidewalk.

Stuart joined Tameka and Ian on the field. "Let her go," he said. "You'll see. Tomorrow she won't argue."

Chapter 9

Stuart was right. The next day at school Jenny didn't argue. But she didn't talk to anyone, either. At lunch she sat by herself at a table on the far side of the cafeteria.

Tameka, Ian, Krishnan and the others sat at their regular table, eating their lunches out of brown paper bags and lunch boxes.

"She must be really mad," Krishnan said.

"So?" Stuart asked. "Let her be mad. Then she'll learn her lesson."

"What lesson is that?" Tameka asked sharply. "Not to argue? Or that you can't trust your friends?"

"I don't see what the big deal is," Stuart said. "This happens in the major leagues all the time. If a player gets lazy or doesn't do what he's supposed to, the manager benches him for a few games."

Krishnan smirked. "This isn't the major leagues."

"It's not even the minor leagues," said Tameka.

"It's not even a *league,*" added Ian.

"Doesn't matter," Stuart insisted.

"That's easy for you to say," Tameka argued. "How would you like it if everyone ganged up on you?"

"I'm not the one who starts fights at every game," Stuart shot back.

"I think we should do what Ian's mom said," suggested Krishnan.

"What's that?" Stuart asked.

"Ask her if something's wrong," Krishnan said. "Like at home or something."

Stuart shook his head doubtfully. "Good luck."

Jenny went outside before they could talk to her. A big group of kids was playing soccer in the school yard, and Jenny joined them. The yard was less than half the size of a regular soccer field and there were a lot of kids, so the game was really crowded.

Ian and the others went outside and watched. Jenny was running around and laughing. It didn't look like anything was bothering her at all. When she saw her friends standing on the side, she wrinkled her nose at them, then turned away and ran after the ball.

"Who's going to talk to her?" Tameka asked.

"I will," Krishnan said, and walked into the soccer game. Since it was a school yard game, no one cared. Kids came and went all the time.

Krishnan and Jenny stood in the middle of the school yard and talked while the soccer game went on around them. A couple of times Jenny turned and looked at Ian, Tameka and Stuart. Once she even kicked the soccer ball as it rolled past her.

Finally, Krishnan came back.

"What'd she say?" Ian asked.

"She's mad that we had a game yesterday and didn't tell her," Krishnan reported.

"Did you explain why we didn't tell her?" Stuart asked.

"She said it wasn't her fault," Krishnan replied. "We made a rule that there'd be a do-over if there was a fight over a call. She just thinks if you make a rule, you should stick to it."

"But she was calling foul tips when there weren't any," Stuart said.

"I didn't bring that up," Krishnan said. "I didn't

want to have another fight. I also told her we were probably going to play today and she should come."

"What'd she say?" Tameka asked.

"She wasn't sure if she could," Krishnan said. "But I got the feeling she was glad I asked."

"Did she say anything about a problem?" Ian asked.

Krishnan shook her head. "She said everything's fine."

Just then, Ms. Jackson came over to the soccer game. She taught fifth grade was Ian's and Krishnan's teacher.

"Jenny!" she called.

In the middle of the soccer game, Jenny stopped and turned.

"Your mother is in the office," Ms. Jackson said. "You have to go."

Jenny frowned, then started across the school yard toward the doors.

"If everything's fine," said Tameka, "how come her mother's in the office?"

Chapter 10

Jenny didn't come to the after-school baseball game that afternoon.

"You know she wanted to be here," Tameka said as they got ready to play.

"Something must be going on," speculated Krishnan.

"Forget about her," Stuart said. "Let's play ball."

The game started. Ian was taking practice swings by the backstop when he heard a plinking sound as if a pebble had hit the metal fencing.

He didn't think much of it. But a few moments later he heard a louder *clank!* A rock about the size of a golf ball fell near his feet.

Ian quickly looked over at the high school parking lot. Four high school kids were picking up rocks and throwing them. Billy, Jenny's stepbrother, was one of them.

Clank! Another rock hit the backstop. Without a word the baseball players picked up their gloves and bats and jogged toward right field. Soon they were standing in a group, beyond the reach of even the strongest rock thrower. Of course, that didn't stop the high school kids from trying. Billy took a running start and hurled one rock so far that it almost *did* reach them.

"Wow," said Stuart. "What an arm."

"Why do they have to break up our game?" Tameka asked. "What's wrong with them?"

"They're jerks," mumbled Richie Perez.

"You'd think they could find something better to do," Krishnan complained.

"That's the whole point," said Stuart. "They can't find anything better to do."

Billy and his friends threw more rocks. The baseball players waited in silence. To Ian and the others, high school kids throwing rocks wasn't a problem you could solve. You wouldn't dare talk to them and you couldn't fight them. Rock throwing was like rain. You just had to wait for it to end.

It wasn't long before the high school kids realized

they couldn't reach the baseball players. They stopped throwing, but didn't leave the high school parking lot.

"What do we do now?" Stuart asked.

"Want to keep playing?" Krishnan suggested hopefully.

"What if they start throwing rocks again?" asked Tameka.

"Maybe they won't," Richie said.

"I think we should skip it," Ian said. "I don't want to be worried every second that I may get hit in the head with a rock."

The others agreed. The game was over.

Chapter 11

They left through the hole in the right field fence. Out on the sidewalk, the baseball players split up and headed home.

"Not that way," Krishnan said as they started down the sidewalk along Main Street.

"You don't want to go past your parents' store?" Ian guessed.

"All the magazines came in today," Krishnan explained. "If they see me they'll make me put them in the racks."

To avoid the store, they walked along Front Street. They were standing at a corner waiting for the light to change when Tameka said, "This is Jenny's block, you know."

"So?" Stuart said.

"Here's an amazing idea," Tameka said. "What if we went over there?"

Stuart made a face. "Why?"

"Just to make sure she's okay," Tameka said.

"But why?" Stuart said again.

"Because she didn't come to the game," Tameka said.

"I don't come to every game," Stuart said. "No one's ever come to my house to make sure I was okay."

"This is different," said Krishnan. "Her mom came to get her at school today. That's not normal."

The light turned green, but they didn't cross the street. The five-dog lady came up behind them and passed with her dogs on their leashes.

Tameka turned to Ian. "Want to go to Jenny's?"

"We don't even know if she's home," Stuart said.

"What if she thinks we're being nosy?" Ian asked.

"I think she'll feel good that we cared enough to stop by," Krishnan said.

"Why don't we just wait until we see her in school tomorrow?" Stuart asked.

Tameka gave him an impatient look. "You'll never want to go, Stuart." She turned to Ian. "What do you want to do?"

"It can't hurt to go by her house," Ian said. "And it's not like any of us are in a rush to get home. We'd still be playing ball if it wasn't for the big kids."

It was three against one. Stuart knew he wasn't going to win. "Okay." He gave in. "Let's go."

They headed down the block and stopped in front of a small gray house. The little patch of grass in front was growing wild and full of dandelions. The screen door had a tear in it. A toy truck with no wheels and a baby stroller were on the porch.

"Looks like no one's home," Stuart said. The words were hardly out of his mouth when the screen door squeaked open and a large woman with a friendly face came out. When she saw the ball players, she looked puzzled.

"Can I help you?" she asked.

"We're friends of Jenny's," Krishnan replied. "Is everything okay?"

The woman glanced back at Jenny's house for a second, then said, "It's nice of you to ask. I really can't say. It's a private matter."

"Can we go in?" Krishnan asked.

"It's probably not a good idea right now," the woman said. "Why don't you wait until tomorrow and see her at school?" The woman paused and looked at Tameka. "I'm Mrs. Peterson. Don't I know you?"

Tameka quickly shook her head and stepped back behind the others.

The lines in Mrs. Peterson's forehead deepened. "Are you sure? You look awfully familiar."

Tameka shook her head again.

"Is Jenny okay?" Krishnan asked.

"Yes, she's fine," Mrs. Peterson assured them. "And it's very nice you came see her. But she's baby-sitting her little brother right now."

Mrs. Peterson walked past them and started to open the door of her car. Once again, she paused and looked at Tameka. Then she got into her car and drove away.

They watched the car go around the corner and disappear into traffic.

"Well, you heard her," Stuart said. "Jenny's busy baby-sitting. So we might as well go."

Tameka glared at him. "Don't you care about anyone except yourself?"

Stuart's jaw dropped. "Why'd you say that? I didn't do anything."

"That's for sure," Tameka snapped.

Ian thought Tameka was right. Stuart didn't seem to care about Jenny. But he was surprised Tameka had made Stuart feel bad in front of his friends.

"It's not Stuart's fault that we can't see Jenny," he said.

"Yeah!" Stuart blurted.

The corners of Tameka's mouth turned down and she pressed her lips together into a hard, crooked line.

"I guess we'd better go," said Krishnan.

They started back down the block.

"That woman really thought she knew you," Krishnan said to Tameka as they walked.

Tameka stared down at the sidewalk. "Never saw her before in my life."

Chapter 12

The next morning when Krishnan and Ian got to school, Jenny was sitting on the concrete steps. She was by herself with her chin in her hands, looking glum. She didn't even look up when Krishnan and Ian stopped in front of her.

"Hi, Jenny," Ian said.

"Hi," Jenny replied, but stared at the ground.

"What happened yesterday?" asked Krishnan.

"I had to baby-sit," Jenny answered.

"Your mom took you out of school just to baby-sit?" Krishnan asked.

"She had to take my stepdad somewhere," Jenny answered.

"Where?" Ian asked.

"A place where they could help him," Jenny said.

Suddenly Ian had a feeling he knew why Jenny was being a little mysterious. Something was wrong with her stepfather, and she didn't want to talk about it.

"We missed you at the game," Krishnan said.

Jenny nodded, but didn't say anything.

"You didn't really miss much," Ian said. "Your stepbrother and his friends chased us off the field."

Jenny looked up curiously.

"With rocks," Krishnan added.

"Did anyone get hit?" Jenny asked.

Ian shook his head.

"It's just so dumb," said Krishnan. "I mean, why do they have to pick on us?"

"Cause they're big and stupid and it's easier to pick on someone smaller than someone their own size," Jenny said bitterly.

"Hey," Ian said. "Did he say anything when he came home last night?"

"He just goes into his room and listens to music," Jenny answered.

"Have you ever asked him why he throws rocks at us?" asked Krishnan.

Jenny shook her head. "We don't talk much."

An awkward moment passed.

"Think you'll play today?" Krishnan asked.

Jenny just gazed off into space. Ian hated to leave her feeling so bad, but he couldn't think of anything else to do.

"We'll see you later, okay?" Ian said.

Jenny stared away and acted as if she hadn't even heard him.

Chapter 13

Jenny didn't eat with her friends at lunchtime. After lunch, when Ian and Tameka and the others played soccer, she sat by herself on a swing in the little kids' playground.

So Ian was both surprised and glad when she showed up at the baseball game after school. The other good news of the day was that Billy and his friends weren't around. Ian picked Jenny for his team and put her in left field. Jenny walked slowly to the outfield.

The game started with Richie Perez batting first for Stuart's team.

Ian was pitching. He wound up and threw. *Crack!* Richie hit the ball hard. Ian watched it sail toward left center. He expected to see Jenny running to catch it, but she was just standing in left field, staring off toward the street.

"Jenny!" Ian shouted.

Jenny turned and looked surprised. She started to run after the ball, but it was too late. Richie was already on his way to second base. Jenny got to the ball and threw it back just as Richie crossed the plate. The rest of his team cheered his home run.

When the inning ended, Jenny walked in from left field with her eyes fixed on the ground.

"Don't worry about it," Ian said. "You're batting third."

Jenny went off and sat by herself until it was her turn at the plate.

Stuart was pitching. When it Jenny's turn to bat, Stuart held the ball and looked at Ian.

"What are we going to do if she starts calling foul tips?" he asked.

"Just pitch it," Jenny grumbled. She stepped into the batter's box and pulled her bat back.

"Jenny?" someone called. Everyone turned. Mrs. Long, Jenny's mom, was hurrying toward them from the parking lot. "What are you doing here? You know you're supposed to be home. I'm late for work."

Jenny ignored her and kept the bat on her shoulder. "Come on, Stuart. Pitch."

Stuart gave Ian a questioning look.

Ian shook his head.

By now Mrs. Long reached the baseball diamond. "Jenny, didn't you hear me?"

"I heard you," Jenny muttered angrily. She glared at Stuart. "Just one pitch."

Again, Stuart gave Ian a questioning look. This time Ian nodded.

Stuart wound up and threw.

Swish! Jenny swung as hard as she could . . . and missed.

Thump! She threw the bat down on the ground and turned to her mother. "Are you happy now?"

"I don't know what you're talking about," Mrs. Long said. "But come on. You have to go home and watch Peter."

Jenny followed her mother off the field and towards the parking lot.

"We can play without her," Stuart said when she'd left.

"I think we should try to find out what's going on," Tameka said.

Stuart frowned. "You just heard what's going on. Her mom said she has to baby-sit."

"She didn't used to have to baby-sit," Krishnan said. She turned to Tameka. "Come on, let's go see."

Krishnan and Tameka began to leave the field.

Stuart couldn't believe it. "Hey!" he yelled. "What about the game?"

"It'll have to wait," Tameka yelled back.

Stuart's mouth fell open and he looked at Ian. "I don't get this! Why is the game stopping? Rain is a reason to stop a ball game. Jerks throwing rocks is a reason. But since when do we stop a game because Jenny has to go baby-sit?"

"Since today," Ian answered and threw him the ball. "We can have a catch till they get back."

Chapter 14

Tameka and Krishnan walked quickly through town to Jenny's house. They knocked on the front door, but no one answered.

Krishnan looked in one of the windows. "It doesn't look like anyone's there. And the baby stroller's gone."

"I bet she took her little brother for a walk," Tameka said. "Maybe we can find her."

They headed back into town and were soon on the sidewalk along Main Street.

"There she is," Tameka said. Jenny was on the next block, pushing the stroller slowly and looking in store windows. They caught up to her outside the store Krishnan's parents owned.

"Looking for something?" Tameka asked.

Jenny spun around. "What are you doing here?"

"We were wondering what's going on," Tameka answered.

"Peter is what's going on." Jenny gestured down at the blond-haired boy strapped into the baby stroller. He was sucking happily on a bottle of apple juice.

"He's cute," Krishnan said.

"I know." Jenny rubbed her little brother's head affectionately. "So what happened to the baseball game?"

"It can wait," answered Krishnan.

Tameka tilted her head toward the store window. "Want to go inside?"

"No way," said Krishnan. "If my parents see me, they'll make me work. Let's get out of here."

They went to a small park down the street. Inside, mothers sat on benches with babies in strollers, and little kids played on swings and seesaws.

Jenny took Peter out of the stroller and let him play in the sand box. The three girls sat together on a bench without talking. They watched a mother change a baby's diaper, and other women push children on swings.

Peter picked up a handful of sand and put it in his mouth.

"Oh, no!" Jenny jumped up and hurried toward him.

Krishnan and Tameka watched as their friend tried to explain to the little boy why he shouldn't eat sand.

"It's yucky, Peter," Jenny said.

Peter looked up at her with wide, innocent eyes, his mouth ringed with sand.

Jenny used the tail of her shirt to wipe the sand away from her brother's mouth. "No more eating sand, okay?" Then she came back to the bench.

"So what's going on?" Tameka asked.

Jenny shrugged. "What does it look like?"

"It looks like you'd rather be playing baseball," Krishnan said.

"Duh."

"But he is cute," Tameka added.

"I know," Jenny admitted. "It's even fun to play with him sometimes. But not every day. It's not fair."

Krishnan understood. All the other baby-sitters on the playground were mothers or grown up ladies. Jenny was the only one under the age of 16. Krishnan had jobs she had to do for her family, but nothing as serious as being a full-time after-school baby-sitter.

"Can't your mom get someone else to baby-sit?" Tameka asked.

Jenny slouched a little lower on the bench and crossed her arms. "We can't afford it."

"Who used to take care of Peter?" Krishnan asked.

"She did," Jenny said. "But that was when my stepdad had a job. Now it's different."

"He lost his job?" Krishnan guessed.

"Sort of," Jenny answered mysteriously.

"He has a problem, right?" Tameka said.

Jenny looked surprised. "You know?"

"We came to your house the other day," said Tameka. "When Mrs. Peterson was there."

Jenny raised her eyebrows. "You know her?"

Tameka nodded. "She works at the treatment center."

"Now I remember," said Krishnan. "She said you looked familiar."

"I pretended I didn't know her because I didn't want to make a big deal out of it," Tameka explained. "But she helped our neighbors, the Smiths, when their son got in trouble."

"What kind of trouble?" Krishnan asked.

"He was on drugs," Tameka said.

Krishnan and Tameka gave Jenny a curious look. Jenny sighed and nodded. "My stepdad, too."

Chapter 15

In the sandbox, Peter put another handful of sand in his mouth.

"Not again!" Jenny groaned and hurried to him.

Tameka and Krishnan shared a look. It wasn't easy to take care of a little kid.

Jenny knelt in front of Peter and wiped his mouth again. "Why do you keep eating sand?"

Instead of answering, the little boy just laughed.

"It must taste pretty good or he wouldn't be eating so much of it," Tameka said.

"Unless he's really hungry," Krishnan added.

"Want a cookie?" Jenny asked her brother.

The little boy nodded.

Jenny brushed the sand off and brought him back

to the bench. She held him on her lap and gave him some cookies.

"Sand and cookies." Tameka wrinkled her nose. "What a combination."

She and Krishnan watched as Jenny gave Peter another bottle of apple juice. The little boy sucked it down eagerly.

"So what's going to happen?" Krishnan asked.

"I don't know," Jenny answered. "My mom really can't earn enough money by herself, and she doesn't know what to do about Billy."

"The rock thrower?" Tameka said.

"He skips school all the time and stays out late," Jenny said. "My mom can't control him."

"But we always see him at the high school," Krishnan said.

"Right," Jenny smirked. "He skips school all day and then goes after school to hang out with his friends. Go figure."

Peter slid off Jenny's lap and wobbled back to the sandbox.

"No more eating sand," Jenny reminded him.

"That's really bad," Krishnan said. "I mean, about your stepdad."

"I just wish I didn't have to baby-sit all the time," Jenny said. "I mean, Saturdays and Sundays and a lot of school days, too. I don't even know when I'll have time to do my homework."

In the sandbox, Peter picked up another handful of sand. He held it up and looked at Jenny. Then he slowly started to bring it toward his mouth.

"You scamp!" Jenny hopped off the bench and got to him just before he could put the sand in his mouth.

"Okay, that's it, Peter boy." Jenny started to tickle him. Peter dropped the handful of sand and began to giggle. But as soon as she tried to take him out of the sandbox, he started to cry and kick.

It was a struggle to hold the crying boy. She brought him back to the stroller, but Peter fought and kicked so hard that she had to ask Krishnan and Tameka for help.

Krishnan was amazed at how strong the little boy was. He kicked and squirmed like a wild animal. Jenny finally managed to strap him into the stroller, but he was really wailing and tears streamed out of his reddened eyes.

The women sitting near them began to mutter and whisper among themselves. Krishnan wondered if they were criticizing the way Jenny handled her little brother, or that a girl Jenny's age had been left in charge of the little boy.

Jenny started to push the stroller out of the park. Peter kept crying and crying. Krishnan felt uncomfortable. She knew Jenny was doing the best job she could, but she also saw how hard it was. Compared to Jenny, Krishnan hardly knew anything about taking care of a little kid.

As she pushed the stroller, Jenny turned to her friends. "Listen, don't tell anyone except Ian about my stepdad, okay? I mean, my mom really doesn't want people to know."

Tameka and Krishnan nodded. Jenny started down the sidewalk, talking softly to Peter.

"Call me tonight, okay?" Tameka called behind her.

"Me, too," said Krishnan.

"Sure," Jenny said without looking back.

Tameka turned to Krishnan. "Think she'll call?"

Krishnan shook her head.

Chapter 16

Krishnan and Tameka walked back to the baseball field.

"All right!" Stuart cheered when he saw them. "Let's play ball!"

"What happened?" Ian asked the girls.

"Do we have to talk about this now?" Stuart asked impatiently.

"Can't you just wait one second?" Tameka asked back, then turned to Ian. "Jenny has to baby-sit her little brother while her mom works. They can't afford anyone else. That's why her mom came and got her today."

Ian could understand. His own parents had gotten divorced when he was four and the Mad Bomber was one. His mom had gone to work and finding a sitter was always a big problem.

"Then it's settled," Stuart said. "Let's play."

Tameka gave him a hard look, but didn't say anything more.

They chose new teams. Ian's team started in the field while Stuart's team batted. Ian was pitching. The first batter on Stuart's team was Richie Perez. Ian waited on the pitcher's mound while Richie took a few warm-up swings.

Thud! Something hit the ground near Ian. He looked down and saw a large rock roll to a stop at his feet. Looking over at the high school parking lot, he saw Billy bend down to pick up another rock. Some of Billy's friends were laughing and shouting encouragement.

"Look out!" Ian yelled at the same moment Billy hurled the next rock. At third base, Krishnan looked up just in time to jump out of the way.

Once again, the baseball players retreated to right field where the rocks couldn't reach them.

"Let's throw some rocks back," suggested Richie.

"Yeah," Stuart quickly agreed. "There are more of us than them. Let's see how they like it."

He started to bend down to find a rock.

"No," Ian said firmly.

Stuart straightened up. "Why not?"

"They're bigger than us," Ian said. "They can throw farther. If we get into a rock war with them, we're guaranteed to lose."

"They probably want us to throw rocks," added Tameka.

"Great," Stuart grumbled. "So now what do we do?"

It was disappointing, but Ian knew the answer.

"We go home," he said. "What else?"

Chapter 17

A little while later Ian let himself into his house. It was dark and empty. In the kitchen, he found a note on the table:

> *Ian—*
> *I have to work late. Give Tommy dinner and keep the door locked. Don't stay up late.*
>
> *Luv You,*
> *Mom.*

He heard the lock on the front door click. That meant Tommy was letting himself in. Ian went to the front hall. He saw a flash of red as his little brother quickly hid something behind his back.

"What's that?" Ian asked.

"Nothing," Tommy answered.

Ian couldn't believe how dumb his brother could be sometimes. "If it's nothing, how come you're hiding it behind your back?"

Tommy didn't answer. His eyes darted left and right as if he was trying to figure out how to escape.

"Come on, Tommy, let's see it." Ian held out his hand.

"Promise you won't take it?" Tommy asked.

"I'm not promising anything," Ian answered. "Now show it to me or else."

Tommy took a red stick out from behind his back. It was about a foot long and an inch thick. The word "DANGER" was written on it in square black letters.

"Now I can blow up the whole block!" he announced.

Ian felt the blood drain out of his face. "Where'd you get that?"

"Found it," Tommy said.

"Where?" Ian asked.

"Where they're digging the big hole," answered Tommy.

Two streets away a construction crew had dug up half a block to pour a foundation for a new building. Ian often paused there to watch the bulldozers move the earth and the pile drivers slam long metal beams into the ground. He had also seen the truck with the words "DANGER—HAZARDOUS MATERIALS—EXPLOSIVES" written in big square letters on the side. The same kind of letters that spelled "DANGER" on the stick Tommy was holding.

"You better give me that," Ian said.

"No!" Tommy quickly hid the red stick behind his back again. "It's mine! I found it!"

"It says 'danger' on it," Ian said. "It could kill you."

Tommy shook his head excitedly. "I know what to do with it."

"What?" Ian asked.

Tommy's eyes darted back and forth again. It was obvious that he had no idea what he was going to do with it. "I'm . . . I'm gonna blow something up."

Ian believed him, but chances were good that the only thing Tommy would blow up was Tommy.

Ian lunged forward and tried to grab the stick out of his little brother's hand. Tommy jumped away, then spun around, and shot back out the front door.

"Come back!" Ian shouted. He dashed outside. Tommy was already two houses away and running down the sidewalk as fast as he could.

Ian got to the sidewalk and started to chase his brother. Ahead of him, Tommy turned the corner and disappeared. A moment later Ian reached the corner. He turned and ran right into the five-dog lady.

Woof! Woof!

Yap! Yap!

The next thing Ian knew, he was tangled in a web of long leashes. The dogs were all around him, barking like crazy.

"Why don't you watch where you're going?" the five-dog lady yelled at him.

Meanwhile, Tommy was halfway down the block, still running with the red stick in his hand. Ian imagined his brother tripping and falling, the stick hitting the ground and blowing up. He imagined Tommy disappearing in a cloud of smoke and flame.

Then Ian imagined trying to explain to his mom what happened: "Tommy found a stick of dynamite. He ran away before I could stop him. Then he fell down and blew himself up."

His mom would kill him.

"Stop!" Ian shouted as he tried to untangle himself from the five-dog lady's leashes. "Someone stop him!"

Down the block, a familiar looking guy stepped out

of a store. He heard Ian's shout. Tommy was just running past when the guy reached out to grab him. Tommy dodged the guy and kept running.

The next thing Ian knew, the guy started to chase his little brother. Ian felt a shock as he realized who that guy was.

It was Jenny's stepbrother, Billy the rock thrower!

Chapter 18

Woof! Woof!

Yap! Yap!

The dogs around Ian were still barking. Ian was still trying to untangle himself from their leashes.

"If you kids weren't in such a rush all the time, this wouldn't happen," the five-dog lady complained.

"Sorry," Ian apologized. "I was just trying to stop my brother from blowing himself up."

"What?" The five-dog lady looked at him like he was crazy.

Ian finally got out of the leashes and dashed down the block. He turned the corner and kept running. Finally, after turning onto another block, he found Jenny's stepbrother holding Tommy.

"Let go!" Tommy struggled to get out of the high schooler's grasp, but Billy was too strong. Ian noticed his little brother's elbow was bleeding.

As Ian got closer, he could see the look of recognition in Billy's face. Billy must've just realized that Ian was one of the baseball players he threw rocks at.

Ian stopped a few feet away. For a moment, he and Billy just stared at each other.

"Let go!" Tommy kept struggling to get out of Billy's grasp.

"Thanks for stopping him," Ian said to Billy.

Billy held on to Tommy. "What's the problem?"

Ian pointed at the red stick in Tommy's hand. "I was afraid he'd blow himself up with that thing."

Billy yanked the red stick out of Tommy's hand.

"Hey! That's mine!" Tommy cried unhappily.

"You were worried about this?" Billy smiled. "It's just a road flare."

"Oh." Ian was surprised. "It said 'danger' on it. I thought it was a stick of dynamite or something."

Billy laughed. "It's just an empty tube. Here."

He tossed the flare to Ian, who caught it. It felt lighter than he expected. Just like an empty cardboard tube.

"It's still mine!" Tommy tried to grab it back, but Ian kept it away from him.

"What happened to your elbow?" Ian asked.

"I fell." Tommy looked at his elbow. He seemed surprised when he saw how much blood there was. Two long ribbons of red ran from his elbow to his wrist, then dripped off.

"We'd better fix that," Ian said.

"You can come to my house," Billy said. "It's just down the block."

Ian looked around and realized they were on Front Street. He would have preferred going home, but he wanted to take care of Tommy's cut before it bled all over his clothes.

"Here's the deal, Tommy," Ian said. "I'll give the tube back, but only if you come with us."

"Deal," Tommy said.

Ian handed his little brother the empty tube. The three of them started down the sidewalk.

"You guys are wrong," Tommy said as he followed behind Ian and Billy. "I can blow up half a block with this. I can blow up the world!"

"Good," Ian said. "Just don't do it until after we fix your elbow."

"Okay," Tommy said. "But then you'll see."

Chapter 19

They walked the rest of the way to Jenny's house without talking. In his mind, Ian kept replaying what had happened with Billy. It seemed so strange that the same kid who threw rocks at him had helped him catch Tommy.

They arrived at the small gray house and went through the gate and past the little patch of grass in front. The screen door squeaked loudly when Billy pushed it open. Inside the house, toy blocks and plastic trucks were scattered around the floor. The smell of hot dogs reminded Ian that he was hungry.

Jenny and Peter were sitting in the living room watching TV.

"What are you doing here?" Jenny asked when Ian and Tommy came in.

Ian told her how Tommy had fallen down and cut his elbow.

"You better come with me," Jenny said to Tommy. She jumped to her feet. "Could you guys watch Peter for a moment?"

Billy and Ian sat down on the couch and watched TV with Jenny's little brother while Jenny led Tommy to the bathroom and cleaned up his cut. Ian still couldn't believe he was sitting in Jenny's living room watching TV with the leader of the rock throwers.

After a while, Jenny and Tommy came back. Jenny had washed the blood off of his arm and had taped a thick white adhesive pad over his elbow.

"Guess what?" Tommy said. "Jenny says we can have dinner here."

"You sure?" Ian asked Jenny, thinking of all the work she probably had to do.

"It's just hot dogs," Jenny replied.

They followed her into the kitchen, which was pretty messy. Dirty dishes were piled in the sink and open cans cluttered the counter top.

"What do you want to drink?" Billy asked while Jenny put Peter in his high chair.

"Got any soda?" Tommy asked.

Billy opened the refrigerator and took out a big

bottle of cola. Tommy grinned at his older brother. Ian knew what he was thinking—at home their mom always made them drink milk at dinner.

Jenny put plates, a bowl of baked beans, and a dish of hot dogs on the table. She bustled around the kitchen just like Ian's mom sometimes did. She cut Peter's hot dog into bite-size pieces, and wiped his face when he smeared baked beans on it.

As they ate, Ian noticed that neither she nor Billy said a word to each other.

The phone rang. Jenny was in the middle of mopping up some soda Peter had spilled on the floor. Ian thought Billy would answer it, but he didn't budge from the table.

Jenny gave Billy an angry look and then got up and answered the phone. "Oh, hi," she said. "Yes, he's here." Jenny held the phone out to Billy. "It's Mom."

With a slight groan, Billy slid his chair back and took the phone. He listened for a moment, and then got angry.

"That's bull!" he growled sharply. "I was at school all day . . . Principal Webber doesn't know what he's talking about . . . Go ahead, let the whole world know! See if I care!"

Billy slammed down the phone and stomped out of the kitchen.

Bang! They heard the screen door slam.

Startled by the commotion, Peter began to whimper. Jenny gathered him into her arms and rocked him gently.

"It's okay, Peter boy. Everything's okay," Jenny said softly.

"Is Billy gonna come back?" Tommy asked with his mouth half-full of hot dog.

"Who cares?" Jenny answered with a shrug.

"You don't like him, do you?" Tommy said.

"He's part of this family, but he never helps," Jenny complained. "When Mom's not home, I have to do everything."

Ian felt bad for her. At home, Tommy didn't help enough, but he was only six, and at least he helped a little.

They finished eating. The dinner table was covered with dirty plates and glasses. Ian looked over at the sink and winced. He knew if he offered to help clean up, in would mean washing all the dirty dishes in the sink, too.

Then Ian smelled something and looked at Peter in

the high chair. Jenny's little brother had a big grin on his face.

"Oh, great," Jenny muttered and got up. She picked Peter up and carried him into another room.

"She's gonna change him?" Tommy asked in a low voice and wrinkled his nose.

"If she doesn't, who will?" whispered Ian.

Tommy pinched his nose with his fingers. "Want to go?"

Ian did, but he knew he couldn't. Instead, he picked up his plate and glass. "We'll go, as soon as we've cleaned this place up."

Tommy looked around at the mess, then shook his head. "No way!" he whispered.

"Well, I am." Ian started to run the water in the sink over the dirty dishes and pots.

"How am I gonna get home?" Tommy asked.

"Guess you'll just have to wait until I'm finished," Ian said.

Tommy narrowed his eyes at his brother. "No fair!"

Ian smiled.

Tommy got up. "Okay, I'll clear the table, but you're washing the dishes."

Chapter 20

Ian and Tommy had almost finished the dishes by the time Jenny came back into the kitchen with Peter. Her eyebrows rose when she saw what Ian and Tommy had done.

"Oh, gosh! Thanks, guys!" she gasped.

"Hey, thanks for dinner," Ian said as he placed the last wet bowl on the dish rack to dry.

Still carrying Peter, she followed Ian and Tommy to the front door.

"See you in school tomorrow," Ian said.

Jenny nodded, then closed the door behind them. Ian realized she would be alone now with Peter until her mom got home from work.

Ian and Tommy walked down the block. It was

dark now; the street lights were on and through windows they could see people watching TVs.

"Why'd we have to do the dishes?" Tommy grumbled.

"If we didn't, who would?" Ian asked.

"I don't know."

"Think about it," Ian said.

Ahead they saw a figure sitting on the curb under one of the street lights. It was Billy.

"Cross the street," Ian whispered to Tommy.

"Why?" Tommy whispered back.

"He seemed pretty mad before," Ian whispered.

"But he wasn't mad at us," Tommy said in a low voice.

Ian knew that was true, but he also knew that Billy threw rocks at them for no reason. You couldn't be sure what a guy like Billy would do.

"Just cross the street, okay?" Ian hissed. He gave Tommy's sleeve a tug and they crossed to the other sidewalk. But as they passed Billy, he looked up and saw them.

Ian was too nervous to say anything.

"Hey, Billy." Tommy gave Jenny's stepbrother a friendly wave.

Ian bit his lip, wondering how Billy would react.

A crooked smile appeared on Billy's face. He waved back. "You guys going home?"

"Yeah," Tommy answered.

"Don't blow anyone up," Billy said.

Chapter 21

The lights were on when Ian and Tommy got home. Inside, Mrs. Piccolo was pulling off her sweater. Underneath it she was wearing her white nursing outfit.

"Where were you?" she asked with a frown.

"Jeez, Mom, I'm sorry," Ian apologized. "I forgot to call and tell you where we were."

"What happened to your arm, Tommy?" Mrs. Piccolo asked.

Tommy told his mother parts of the story, about how he was running and fell down, and how they had dinner at Jenny's. He skipped the part about the red tube marked "DANGER."

"So how was dinner?" Ian's mom asked.

Tommy and Ian shrugged.

Mrs. Piccolo frowned. "Something wrong?"

"Everybody's mad at everybody in Jenny's house," Tommy said.

Mrs. Piccolo gave Ian a curious look. "Why do you think that is?"

"Jenny's stepdad has a problem," Ian said. "I'm not supposed to tell anyone. But now her mom has to go to work and Jenny has to baby-sit. And her stepbrother Billy keeps skipping school and getting into trouble."

"Isn't he the one who throws rocks?" his mother asked.

"Yes, but you won't believe what he did," Ian said, then told her the story of how Billy helped stop Tommy and offered to have Tommy come to his house to fix his elbow.

"I mean, he acted nice," Ian said.

Mrs. Piccolo smiled. "Sometimes people aren't what you think they are."

"I'll say," Ian agreed. "But if he's not so bad, how come he throws rocks at us?"

"Why do you think he does it?" his mother asked.

"Gee, Mom, I don't have a clue," Ian said. "Maybe he's just weird."

Mrs. Piccolo smiled. "And maybe you ought to think about it some more."

"You always talk in riddles to me," Ian complained.

"How would I know why he does it? I'm not a mind reader."

"No, but you're a smart boy," Mrs. Piccolo said.

"Well, if you think you know, why don't you tell me?" Ian asked.

"Because I want you to think about it," his mom replied. "Now it's time for you two to get to bed."

Ian and Tommy washed up and went into the bedroom they shared. As usual, Tommy went to sleep right away while Ian stayed up and read a comic under a small reading light.

A little while later his mom tapped lightly on the door and came in. She sat down on the edge of Ian's bed.

"What do you want to do?" she asked in a low voice.

"About what?" Ian asked.

"Do you want to help Jenny and her family?" Mrs. Piccolo asked.

"I don't know," Ian replied uncertainly. "I guess I do. But how?"

"We could invite Jenny and her brothers to come over for dinner," Mrs. Piccolo suggested. "Sometimes just letting someone know other people care makes them feel better. Then they don't feel so alone."

"Jenny shouldn't feel alone," Ian said. "She has friends."

"How many invite her into their homes?" Mrs. Piccolo asked. "You can have all the friends in the world at school, but if no one seems to care outside of school, then you're going to be lonely."

Ian understood what she was saying. But he still felt weird about asking Jenny over for dinner. Well, it wasn't so much Jenny he felt weird about. It was Billy.

"Do we have to invite Billy, too?"

"You don't have to do anything," his mom said. "Just think about it. It could be a very nice gesture. You can tell them they're not the only ones who've eaten here. Stuart and Krishnan have been here, too."

Ian knew she was right. But inside he still felt strange. What if they invited Billy and he brought a rock?

Chapter 22

The next day in school, Ian saw Jenny in the hall, but he didn't ask her to come for dinner. It would have been a lot easier to ask if she wanted to have a catch or something.

"Did you tell Jenny about the game?" Krishnan asked that afternoon at the baseball field. She and Ian were standing behind the backstop. Richie Perez was up at bat. The high school parking lot was empty. Billy and his rock-throwing friends weren't around.

"She has to baby-sit," Ian answered.

"Too bad," Krishnan said. "We could use her today."

"My mom wants me to invite her and Billy over for dinner," Ian said. "So they feel like people care."

Crack! Richie hit a line drive straight up the middle. Out in center field, Tameka scooped up the ball and threw it to second base. Richie was held to a single.

The next batter went up to the plate. Ian's thoughts went back to Jenny.

"There's just one thing," he said. "I tried to ask her, but I couldn't."

"Why not?" asked Krishnan.

"I don't know." Ian shrugged. "It just felt weird."

"Like you were asking if she wanted to go out?" Krishnan guessed.

Ian felt his face grow warm and turn red.

Krishnan smiled. "You want me to ask her for you?"

Ian sort of nodded. "For dinner, not to go out."

"Yes, Ian." Krishnan grinned. "I got that."

Chapter 23

The next day, Ian was waiting in the lunch line when Jenny came up to him.

"Sounds great," she said. "When?"

It took Ian a moment to realize she was talking about dinner. "How about tonight?"

"I'll check with my mom," Jenny said. "She's working the day shift today. She might want me to eat at home."

Jenny went to the office to call her mom. A little while later she came back to the cafeteria.

"She said it's fine and thank you," she told Ian. "She wants to take Peter to the second-hand store and see if they have anything that'll fit him."

"What about Billy?" Ian asked.

"I'll tell him if I see him," Jenny said.

• • •

That afternoon, for the first time in a week, Jenny played in the after-school baseball game. Over in the high school parking lot, Billy was hanging out with some of his friends. Halfway through the baseball game, Jenny went over and talked to him.

"What'd he say?" Ian asked when she came back.

"He'll think about it," she answered.

Jenny played the whole game and didn't argue once. When the game ended, she hurried over to Ian.

"Ready?" she asked eagerly.

They left the baseball field together. Billy wasn't around. Ian was still surprised that Jenny seemed so happy to have dinner with him.

"I was just wondering," he said as they walked through town. "What did Krishnan tell you?"

"She said your mom makes the best garlic bread in the world," Jenny answered.

"That's all?"

"She's jealous that I got invited," Jenny said. "She said she wanted to come, too."

Ian smiled to himself. Krishnan was pretty smart.

It wasn't long before they got to Ian's house. But when they reached the front steps, Jenny stopped.

"What's wrong?" Ian asked.

"I'm really not hungry," she said.

That caught Ian by surprise. Just moments before she'd acted like she couldn't wait to come for dinner. Now she was acting like she didn't want to.

"It's not a big deal," Ian said.

"I know," said Jenny. "I just don't feel like it."

She looked up and down the street. Ian thought she was trying to decide which way to go.

"You mean, you're going skip my mom's garlic bread?" he asked.

Jenny looked at him questioningly.

"Listen," Ian said. "We don't have to talk about anything you don't want to talk about. But I called my mom at work and told her you were coming for dinner and that you wanted to try her garlic bread. I bet she's inside making it right now."

Jenny glanced at the front door. She took a deep breath, and then followed Ian inside.

Chapter 24

The house smelled like cooking. In the kitchen, Ian's mom was stirring a big pot. Steam rose from the pot. They were having spaghetti again.

"You must be Jenny," Mrs. Piccolo dabbed a few beads of sweat from her brow caused by the steaming pot. "Is your brother coming?"

"I'm not sure," Jenny replied and glanced warily around the kitchen. "Is that okay?"

"Yes," Mrs. Piccolo said. "I always make too much anyway. Maybe you kids could set the table."

Ian showed Jenny where the plates and silverware were. They put out glasses and milk and grated cheese for the spaghetti.

Tommy came into the kitchen wearing his camouflage clothes. "I'm going outside, Mom."

"Okay, but not too far," his mom said. "We're going to eat soon."

Tommy left the kitchen.

"How was today's ball game?" Mrs. Piccolo asked while Ian and Jenny set the table.

"Great," Ian said. "Stuart and Tameka were captains. Jenny and I were on Tameka's team and we beat them pretty good."

"I'm glad," Mrs. Piccolo said, "but I'm not sure that's proper English. What do you think, Jenny? Should it be 'we beat them pretty good' or 'we beat them pretty well'?"

"I'd just say we slaughtered them," Jenny replied.

Mrs. Piccolo laughed. She and Jenny shared a smile. Then she turned to Ian. "Why don't you go out and keep an eye on Tommy before he blows up the block?"

Ian frowned. "Why?"

"He'll forget to come in for dinner," said Mrs. Piccolo.

"You usually just call him from the window," said Ian.

Mrs. Piccolo gave her son a look. "Go check on him, okay?"

Ian understood. His mom wanted him to go so that she could talk to Jenny.

• • •

"So, Jenny," Mrs. Piccolo said after Ian left, "I hear your stepbrother is causing some problems at your games."

"He's a jerk," Jenny said, dawdling beside a chair.

"Why does he throw rocks?" Mrs. Piccolo asked as she poured the spaghetti and boiling water through a colander. A big cloud of steam rose out of the sink.

"Guess he doesn't have anything better to do," Jenny said.

"And then there's your little brother," said Mrs. Piccolo. "How old is he?"

"Two."

"So sometimes he's cute and lovable and you're crazy about him," said Ian's mom, "and other times he's a pest that makes messes and you wish he'd disappear forever."

Jenny's eyebrows rose in surprise. "How'd you know?"

"I have a little brother, too," said Ian's mom. "I mean, he's thirty-five now and not so little anymore. But I had to baby-sit him when we were young."

"Didn't you hate it?" Jenny asked.

"I can't say it was always fun," Mrs. Piccolo admitted. "But I didn't have a choice."

"Did you have to baby-sit him almost every day and on the weekends?" Jenny asked.

"No," Mrs. Piccolo said. "Only sometimes."

"I don't know any other kid who has to baby-sit as much as me," Jenny complained. "Everyone else gets to play after school. It's not fair."

"You're right," Mrs. Piccolo agreed. She dumped the colander of spaghetti into a big bowl and poured spaghetti sauce over it. "So, what do you think you can do?"

Jenny shrugged.

"Maybe you don't want to talk about it," Mrs. Piccolo said.

Jenny didn't respond. The truth was, she didn't know. Ian's mom wiped her hands on a dish towel.

"It must be hard," she continued. "But everyone goes through some rough times in their life."

Jenny gave Mrs. Piccolo a quizzical look. She hardly knew this lady. All she knew was that she was Ian's mom. Well, and that she seemed nice. "Have you?"

"Well, let's see," Mrs. Piccolo said. "I've been through two divorces."

"You've been divorced twice?" Jenny asked.

"No, I went through it once when my parents got divorced and once when I got divorced," Mrs. Piccolo explained.

"How come your parents got divorced?" Jenny asked.

"They just couldn't get along," Mrs. Piccolo said. "Then after the second time—when I got divorced—I had two little kids and I had to work. Just like your mom. I didn't have anyone to take care of them. So I had to put them in day care. The people at the day care center were nice enough, but they had a lot of kids to look after. I wish I'd had someone like you, Jenny. Someone who was part of the family to help take care of them."

"But that's what isn't fair," Jenny said. "I'm just a kid. Peter's not my baby. Why should I have to watch him every day after school?"

"Believe me, hon, your mom didn't plan it this way," Mrs. Piccolo said. "Sometimes things happen that you don't expect. Your mom's doing the best she can. She just doesn't have any other choice right now."

"How do you know?" Jenny asked.

Mrs. Piccolo smiled. "Because she's your mother, and I'm sure she doesn't want you to be unhappy."

Jenny gazed curiously at Ian's mom. She sensed that she was probably right.

"One way or another it's going to work out," Mrs. Piccolo said. "The important thing to remember is that your mom loves you and wants to take care of you. That's why she's out working. It's not like you're the only one in the family who's struggling with this."

Jenny knew that part was true. She stared down at the kitchen table and then looked back up. "What happened to your husband?"

"He lives over in Springdale," Mrs. Piccolo said. "He has dinner with the boys on Wednesday nights, and they go to his house every other weekend and on some vacations, too."

"Does he have a new wife?" Jenny asked.

"Yes," Mrs. Piccolo answered. "And they even have a couple of kids of their own. But he still makes time to see Ian and Tommy."

"I bet his new wife doesn't like that," Jenny said.

Mrs. Piccolo smiled. "You may be right. But it wouldn't surprise me if she understands. After all, she knows what it's like because she's got two kids of her own. So I hope she understands that Ian's dad now has four kids. Ian and Tommy are still his sons and he still loves them."

"How come you want him to see Ian and Tommy if you don't like him anymore?" Jenny asked.

"I'm not seeing him," Mrs. Piccolo said with a laugh, "they are. What about your real father, Jenny?"

Jenny shook her head. "I don't know. I never met him and Mom never talks about him. I'm pretty sure he and my mom never got married."

"That happens," Mrs. Piccolo said.

"Do you ever think about getting back together with your husband?" Jenny asked.

"I used to wonder about it," Ian's mom said. "Of course, it's too late now. I'm just glad the boys get to see him."

The front door slammed and they heard footsteps coming down the hall.

"They did too use nuclear bombs in Vietnam," Tommy insisted loudly.

"No way," said Billy.

Ian, Tommy and Jenny's stepbrother entered the kitchen. Ian and Tommy had run into Billy on the side-walk.

"You must be Billy," Mrs. Piccolo said.

Billy nodded a little awkwardly.

"Mom, didn't they drop nuclear bombs in Viet-nam?" Tommy asked.

Mrs. Piccolo thought for a moment, then shook her head. "No, Tommy, I don't think so."

Billy grinned. "See, wise guy?"

Tommy's forehead wrinkled with confusion. "But they used them in World War Two, and that was way before Vietnam."

"That's true," Mrs. Piccolo said.

"Then why didn't they use them in Vietnam?" Tommy asked.

"I'm not sure I know the precise reason," Mrs. Piccolo answered. "I'd like to think that they knew too many innocent people would be killed."

"What's wrong with that?" asked Tommy.

Mrs. Piccolo sighed and shook her head. She didn't understand what her younger son was going through. But whatever it was, she just hoped he'd get through it *soon.*

Chapter 25

They didn't talk about anything serious during dinner, just movies and TV shows and stuff like that. Billy had seconds and then thirds. You would have thought he hadn't eaten in weeks. Ian still couldn't believe that the same kid who threw rocks at them was now sitting at dinner acting like it was the most normal thing in the world.

To Ian, the most interesting part of the evening was when his mom asked Billy if he'd ever played baseball.

"I used to play all the time," Billy answered.

"Really?" Jenny asked, surprised.

"Don't you two live under the same roof?" Ian's mom asked in a teasing way.

Jenny looked at her stepbrother. "How come you never told me?"

"You never asked," Billy answered.

"Do you still play?" Mrs. Piccolo asked Billy.

"Not really," Billy said. "None of my friends are into it."

"Have you asked them?" Ian's mom asked.

"Well, no," Billy admitted.

Ian expected his mom to ask more questions, but she didn't. She was funny that way. Sometimes she'd ask just enough questions to get you thinking about something. Then she'd leave you to figure out the rest on your own.

Dinner ended.

"Want to see my collection of bullets?" Tommy asked Billy.

"They're just empty shells," Ian explained.

"Are not!" Tommy insisted. "They're totally real."

Billy got the message. "Sure."

He and Tommy went upstairs.

"How's that for two peas in a pod?" Mrs. Piccolo asked with a smile.

"Hard to believe," Ian said.

"Thanks for dinner. It was really good," Jenny said, getting up. "I'd better go do my homework."

"You want me to get Billy?" Ian asked.

Jenny shook her head. "It sounds like he's having fun with your brother. He won't care if I walk home alone."

Ian walked with her to the front door.

"Thanks for inviting us," Jenny said.

"Sure," Ian said. "I, er, hope it was okay."

"Your mom's really nice," Jenny said. "And the garlic bread was great. See you at school tomorrow."

"Right." Ian opened the door for her. As Jenny started down the steps, he had a thought. "Hey, Jenny?"

She stopped and looked back at him. "What?"

"If you ever want to come over for dinner again, I'm sure my mom would love it," Ian said. "I mean, and me, too."

Jenny smiled. "Thanks, Ian."

Chapter 26

The next morning Krishnan, Tameka and Ian walked through town toward school.

"Did Jenny eat over last night?" Krishnan asked.

"Yep," Ian said. "And her stepbrother, too."

"The rock-thrower?" Tameka gasped. "Are you serious?"

"Sure am," Ian replied.

"Did you talk to him?" Krishnan asked.

"Just like normal." Ian was still finding it hard to believe.

"So, what's with him?" Tameka asked.

"We didn't talk about that," Ian said. "But guess what? He used to play ball when he was our age. Even Jenny didn't know."

"How did it go with Jenny?" asked Krishnan.

"Okay, I guess," Ian said. "I wasn't there for that part. She and my mom talked alone. All I know is she was in a better mood after that. And believe it or not, Billy and my brother Tommy really got along."

"Hey, guys!" someone called out.

It was Jenny, about half a block behind them, hurrying to catch up. "Think there'll be a game after school?"

"Sure," Ian said. "You can play?"

"Better believe it," Jenny said. "My mom's on the early shift again. Nothing can stop me."

"Except . . ." Tameka was going to say something about the rock throwers, then caught herself.

But it was too late. As if she'd read Tameka's mind, Jenny's face clouded over.

"I'm sorry, Jenny," Tameka apologized.

"Forget it," Jenny replied. "He threw rocks at me, too."

"Maybe after last night he won't," Ian said.

"Don't bet on it," Jenny said. "He's different when he's with his friends."

"Maybe they won't be there," Krishnan said hopefully. "They weren't at the last game."

"But you know they're going to come back sooner or later," said Tameka. "I just wish there was something we could do about them once and for all."

"Know what would be cool?" Ian asked. "We could challenge them to a game."

Krishnan blinked with surprise. "The rock throwers?"

"Sure," Ian said. "Why not?"

"Because they're bigger," Tameka said. "They hit farther and throw harder."

"So?" Ian said. "We'll just play deeper. Besides, it doesn't matter whether we win or not. The idea is we'll get to play without them bothering us."

"Ian's right," Jenny said, suddenly excited. "It could be fun. We should do it."

"We'll need to have all our best players," Ian said, looking at Jenny.

"Hey, no sweat," Jenny said. "I wouldn't miss it for anything."

• • •

"Have you gone psycho?" Stuart gasped at lunch when Ian told him the plan. "They'll kill us!"

"Maybe," Ian said. "But so what?"

Stuart looked to the others to see what they thought.

"I think it's a certified amazing idea of the day," Tameka said.

"It's great," added Jenny.

Ian couldn't believe how excited she was about playing against her stepbrother and the other rock throwers.

"Who's going to ask them?" Stuart wanted to know.

That was a good question. Ian and his friends exchanged nervous looks. It was one thing to talk to Billy when he was alone. But it was quite another to walk up to him in the high school parking lot when he was with his friends.

"I'll do it," Jenny volunteered.

Everyone looked at her like she was crazy.

"Hey, come on," Jenny assured them. "They're not going to beat up a girl."

"I wouldn't be so sure," Stuart warned.

Chapter 27

That afternoon, the baseball players walked over to the high school.

"I really think we can beat them," Jenny said.

"Hold on, Jenny," Tameka said. "We don't even know if they're going to be there."

"But if they are," Jenny said, "we can win. I mean, we play all the time. Do you ever see any of *them* playing ball?"

The others shook their heads.

"This is a switch," Tameka said with a smirk. "Most of the time we pray they won't be there."

When they got to the high school, Billy and his friends were in the parking lot, smoking cigarettes. The baseball players stopped.

"You're in luck, Jenny," Tameka said with a chuckle.

"Yeah," Stuart added. "Here's your big chance. Go ask them." He said it in a way that implied he didn't think she'd have the nerve to do it.

Jenny narrowed her eyes at Stuart, then looked over at the parking lot. She didn't move.

"Change your mind?" Stuart taunted.

"I don't see *you* racing over there," Jenny shot back.

"Hey, I never said I would," Stuart defended himself. "You're the one who wants to play ball with them."

Jenny still didn't go. Ian couldn't blame her. It was a lot easier to talk about going up to the big kids than to actually do it.

"You don't have to do it, Jenny," Krishnan said.

"Yeah," Tameka agreed. "Why don't we just play? Maybe they won't bother us."

Suddenly Jenny started toward the parking lot. Ian watched her go.

"Hey, wait up." He jogged to catch her.

A few seconds later he and Jenny stood in front of Billy and his friends. Even though Ian had been with Billy the night before, he now felt a nervous, sour sensation in his stomach.

The older kids stared down at them.

Jenny slid her hands into her back pockets and stuck her chin out. "You guys want to play ball?"

One of the guys wrinkled his forehead. "What?"

"We're challenging you to a baseball game," Jenny said. "You know how to play baseball, don't you?"

Billy grinned.

"What is this, a joke?" asked a big kid with red hair.

"We're serious," Jenny answered.

"You're whacked," another big guy mumbled.

But Billy must not have thought so because he turned and started to count his friends.

"Are you crazy, Billy?" asked the guy with red hair. "What do you want to play these little creeps for?"

"Why not?" Billy asked back. Then he repeated what Jenny had said: "You know how to play baseball, don't you?"

"This is stupid," the guy with red hair sputtered.

"Afraid they'll beat us?" Billy asked him with a sly grin.

"No way," said another guy.

"Then let's do it," said Billy.

"Drop dead," grumbled the red-haired guy. "I'm out of here." He started to leave the parking lot.

The corners of Billy's mouth turned down. He

looked back at Ian and Jenny. "We don't have enough guys. How about tomorrow? That'll give me time to find some more."

"Sounds good to me," said Jenny.

She and Ian headed back to the field.

"So?" Stuart arched an eyebrow suspiciously when they arrived at the baseball diamond.

"They don't have enough guys," Jenny said.

Stuart grinned. "Good."

"We'll just have to wait until tomorrow," added Ian.

Stuart's mouth fell open. *"Tomorrow?"*

Tameka shook her head in wonder. "This I don't believe."

Chapter 28

The next morning, Ian walked to school with Krishnan and Tameka.

"Today's the big day, I guess." Tameka sounded a little nervous.

"Don't worry," Ian said. "Everything will be fine."

"Did you see how excited Jenny was yesterday?" Krishnan asked.

"Isn't it weird?" said Tameka. "I thought she hated her stepbrother."

"Guess you never know," mused Ian. "They were friendly enough at my house."

When they got to school, Jenny was sitting on the steps with her chin in her hands looking very glum.

"Uh oh, something's wrong," Krishnan said.

Jenny looked up at them. Her eyes were red-rimmed and she looked like she'd been crying. "I can't play today," she said with a sniff. "I have to baby-sit."

"Did you tell your mom about the game?" Tameka asked.

Jenny nodded. "They put her back on the late shift."

Krishnan glanced at Ian. Ian glanced at Tameka. If only there was something they could do.

• • •

At lunch Jenny sat alone at a table on the other side of the cafeteria.

"Why's she mad at *us?*" Stuart asked.

"She's not," said Krishnan. "She just feels bad. You know how sometimes when you feel bad you don't want to be with anyone."

Stuart shook his head. "Not me. I always want to be with people."

"Well, you're different," said Tameka.

"It really stinks she can't play today," said Ian. "She was the most excited of all of us."

They ate in silence for a moment.

"Know what's totally dumb about this?" Stuart

asked. “Why does she have to stay home? If she wants to play baseball, why doesn’t she just bring her little brother to the game? I mean, what’s the big deal? I’ve seen people change little kids’ diapers in public. So what?”

Ian blinked and turned to Krishnan and Tameka. They stared back at him with astonished looks on their faces. Ian knew what they were thinking: the answer was so obvious and simple. Why hadn’t they thought of it sooner?

All at once, Ian, Tameka and Krishnan jumped up.

“Hey!” Stuart said. “What’s going on?”

“You’re a genius, Stuart,” said Krishnan.

“I am?” Stuart asked.

“Just don’t let it go to your head,” added Tameka.

Jenny gave them a puzzled look when they crowded around the table where she was sitting by herself.

“We’ve got the answer,” Krishnan said excitedly and then explained it.

“And it was my idea!” Stuart added proudly.

Jenny shook her head. “It won’t work. Who’ll watch Peter when I’m out in the field?”

“One of us,” said Tameka.

"But you'll be in the field, too," Jenny pointed out.

"Then we'll take turns," said Ian. "We'll each sit out an inning and watch him."

"We will?" Stuart asked. Ian, Krishnan and Tameka glowered at him. "Uh, I guess we will. There's just, er, one thing."

"What?" asked Tameka.

"I'm not changing any diapers," Stuart said.

Chapter 29

That afternoon Billy managed to round up enough guys to make a team. They were a funny sight with their earrings and tattoos. Some of them didn't have baseball gloves, so Ian and his friends lent them theirs.

The game started and it quickly became obvious that some of the big guys knew how to play baseball, while others hardly had a clue. Billy was the best of them.

The game stayed close. The older guys could hit the ball harder and farther than the younger kids. They made so many errors, though, that Ian and his team always managed to catch up during their turn at bat.

Finally, Billy's team won in the bottom of the ninth inning when he hit a grand slam homer with bases loaded. Jenny's stepbrother rounded the bases with his arms raised in triumph while his friends cheered and gave each other high fives. They acted just like every other winning ball team on earth.

Stuart had thrown the pitch that Billy blasted out of the park. Now he stood on the pitcher's mound with his head down.

Ian walked in from second base. "Hey, come on," he said. "It's just a game."

Stuart banged his fist into his glove. "I tried to sneak a fast ball by him. I should've thrown a curve."

"So you'll do it next time," Ian said, patting him on the shoulder.

Stuart scowled at him. "*Next* time?"

"Hey," Ian replied with a wink, "you never know."

They walked over to the backstop where the high school kids were still congratulating each other. Jenny had sat out the last inning because it was her turn to watch Peter.

"Good game," Ian said.

Billy turned to him with a grin. "Yeah, it was cool."

"You wouldn't have won if I was out there," Jenny said.

"Yeah, right," her stepbrother chuckled.

"Maybe we'll play again sometime," Ian said.

Billy nodded. "Sure."

He and his friends started away from the field, still talking loudly about the game.

Ian and his friends watched them go.

"Hard to believe," Tameka said.

"They weren't so great," said Stuart.

"I liked catching the balls they hit a lot more than the rocks they throw," said Richie Perez.

Everyone laughed.

Then, for the first time in a long time, Ian and his friends left the field and walked home across the high school parking lot without being scared.

Chapter 30

For the rest of the spring and into the summer, the baseball players met on the high school field. Evening after evening they played until the sun fell low in the sky and their shadows grew long across the weeds and dirt.

Sometimes Billy and his friends hung around in the parking lot, but now they acted okay.

And they never threw rocks.

Jenny often brought Peter in his stroller. When it was their turn to watch him, Ian and his friends taught him how to throw. It wasn't long before he was a pretty good ballplayer, for a two-year-old.

One summer morning, Jenny came to a game and told everyone her stepfather was out of the treatment center. She said her mom still had to work for a while, but at least things were more peaceful at home.

And now that her stepdad was around, she wouldn't have to bring Peter to the games unless she wanted to.

Like Ian's mom had said, things usually worked out and life kept going on.

And there was always baseball.